Don't Forget to Come Back!

For Sam. For Ella.
Thanks for all the squeezy hugs and noisy kisses!
R. H. H.

For my big sister, Rachel.
H. B.

ISBN: 0-439-85580-2

12 11 10 9 8 7 6 5 4 3 2 1   6 7 8 9 10/0

Printed in the U.S.A.   08

This edition first printing, January 2006

This book was typeset in Alghera.
The illustrations were done in watercolor and ink.

Don't Forget to Come Back!

Robie H. Harris

pictures by Harry Bliss

SCHOLASTIC INC.
New York Toronto London Auckland Sydney
Mexico City New Delhi Hong Kong Buenos Aires

Guess what?
Yesterday Daddy told *me* something very important. He told *me* that he and Mommy were going out right after *supper* — and Sarah was coming to babysit.

I didn't like that one bit!

So I told Daddy three very important things.

I still wanted Daddy and Mommy to stay home with me. So I told Daddy three very scary things.

"1. If you go out tonight, the most giant, most loudest thunderstorm ever will come — and blow our house down!

"2. If you go out tonight, I'll get a very bad tummy ache — and I'll throw up!

"3. And if you go out tonight, the biggest baddest moose will walk into the kitchen — and eat me all up!"

That didn't scare Daddy at all!

I ran and grabbed Panda, a bag of chips,
my bike helmet, my ⌐⌐ my ballet shoes,
my umbr⌐⌐

See, I'm ready to go. And if you really, really love me, you'll take me with you.
We always love you, Pumpkin, even when we go out.

Daddy always calls me Sugar and Mommy always calls me Pumpkin just before they go out. So the bad news was — they were still going out.

Well, if you go out, I won't be nice anymore. And you won't like that!

I was so-ooo mad,
I ran into the closet
and shut the door.

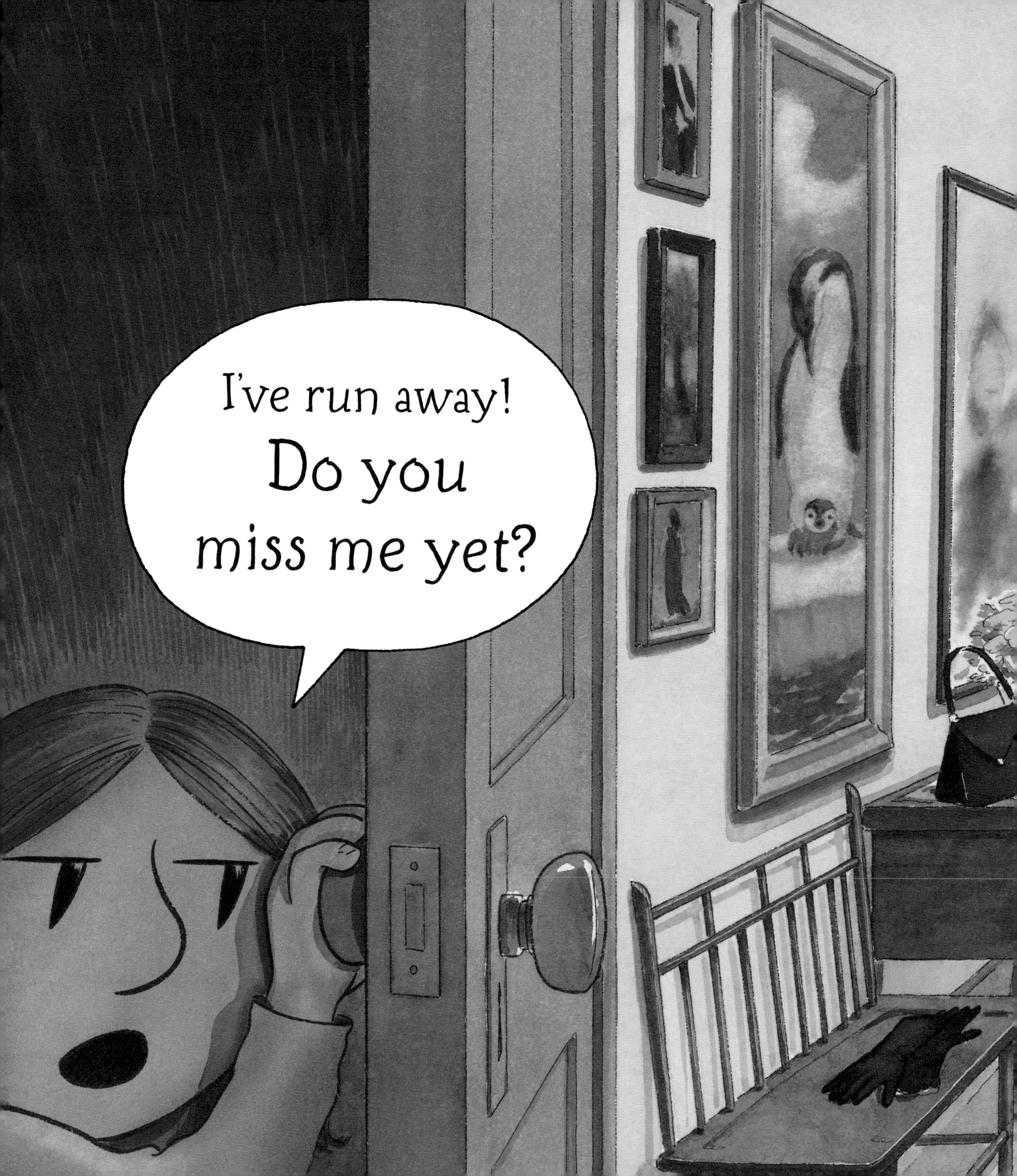
I've run away! Do you miss me yet?

We miss you already, Sugar. Hope you won't be gone forever! Please come home soon.

Well, if you go out, then I'll go somewhere—I don't know where—but somewhere very far away. And maybe, just maybe, I'll never ever come back!

The doorbell rang.
I grabbed Panda and ran to my room.

Guess what? Sarah walked into my room.

I do like Sarah. And she's not stupid. She's silly!

Guess what now? It was time for Daddy and Mommy to go.
So I told them three very important things.

And finally, they went out.

After they left, Sarah and I were so busy we didn't have time to go all the way to the South Pole. Sarah heated up cheese pizza, with pepperoni and pineapple on top.

After that, Sarah let me paint my fingernails and toenails with silver and purple polish.

Then we put orange lipstick on our noses, cheeks, and lips. We looked like clowns, and I liked that.

And before I went to bed, Sarah didn't make me
wash off any of my clown makeup. I liked that, too.
And she read me my monster book — five times!
That was so-ooo cool.

Guess what else? This morning, when I tiptoed into Daddy and Mommy's room, there they were — asleep and snoring in the big bed.

I gave them squeezy hugs and noisy kisses — and they both woke up.

And when they saw me, they were so happy I didn't forget to come back — all the way from the South Pole. So I told them three more very important things.

1. The South Pole is too cold.

2. Sarah is so-ooo silly!

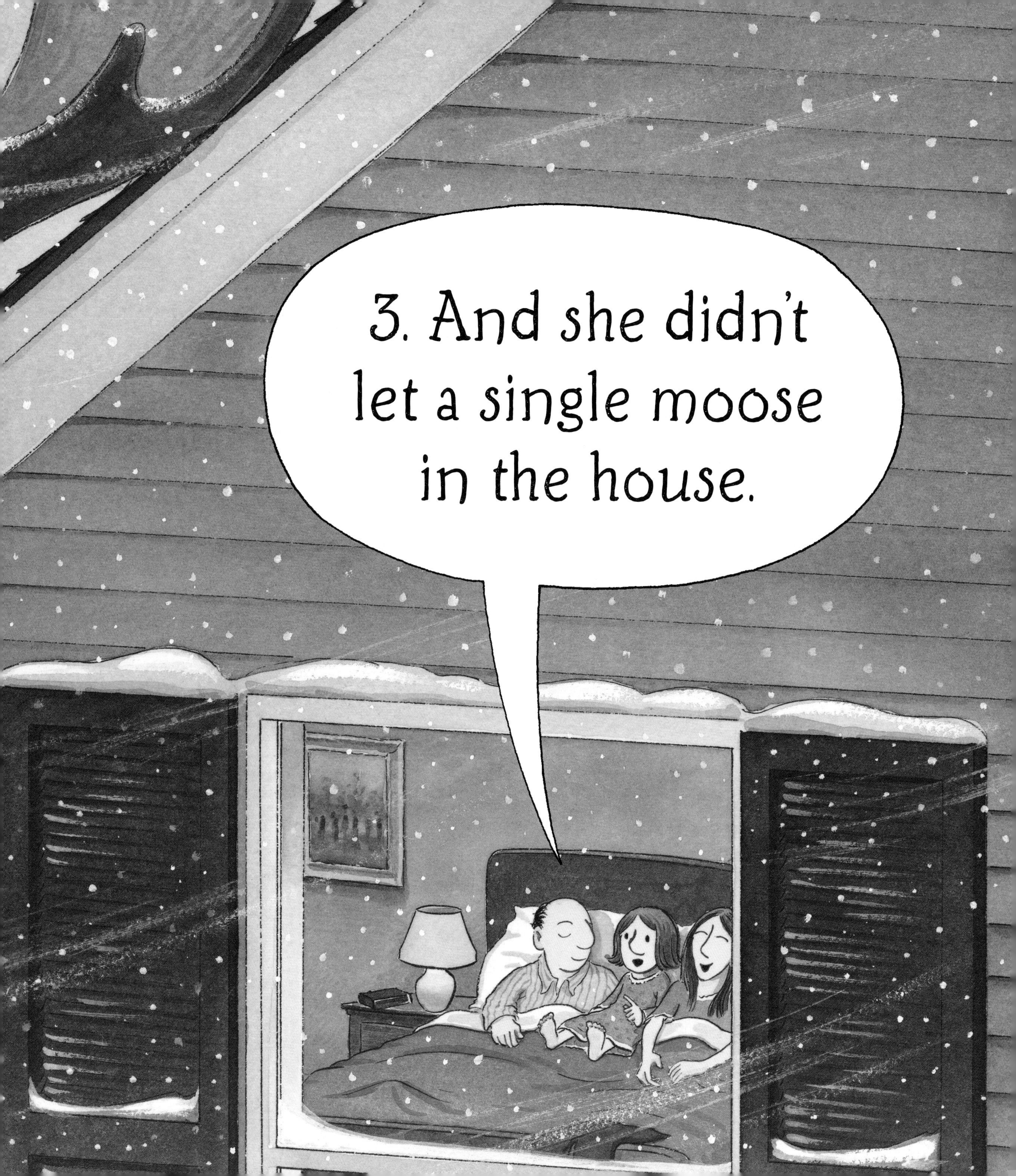
3. And she didn't let a single moose in the house.